T0269873

THE VANISHING PLACE

THERESA EMMINIZER

An imprint of Enslow Publishing

WEST **44** BOOKS™

Please visit our website, www.west44books.com.
For a free color catalog of all our high-quality books,
call toll free 1-800-542-2595 or fax 1-877-542-2596.

Cataloging-in-Publication Data

Names: Emminizer, Theresa.
Title: The vanishing place / Theresa Emminizer.
Description: New York : West 44, 2020. | Series: West 44
 YA verse
Identifiers: ISBN 9781538385081 (pbk.) | ISBN
 9781538385098 (library bound) | ISBN 9781538385104
 (ebook)
Subjects: LCSH: Children's poetry, American. | Children's
 poetry, English. | English poetry.
Classification: LCC PS586.3 V365 2020 | DDC
 811'.60809282--dc23

First Edition

Published in 2020 by
Enslow Publishing LLC
101 West 23rd Street, Suite #240
New York, NY 10011

Editor: Caitie McAneney
Designer: Seth Hughes

Photo Credits: Cover (sky) ANTIVAR/Shutterstock.com;
cover (water) Dmitry Laudin/Shutterstock.com; cover
(mountain) nasidastudio/Shutterstock.com; cover (raft)
Giangiacomo Rocco/Shutterstock.com.

Printed in the United States of America

CPSIA compliance information: Batch #CW20W44: For further information contact
Enslow Publishing LLC, New York, New York at 1-800-542-2595.

For Ian, my adventure partner, and Rachael, my confidant.

Brooke

It Started

with a *yes*.

A *yes*
that slipped
easily
from my lips.

*Would you girls want to
    meet up later?*

        We could all go out
on Nate's dad's boat?

Jay's green eyes
were both
        nervous and eager.

His voice was
low and soft.

        Like the moon

                s u s p e n d e d

over the water.

A small doubt
like a mosquito
tickled the back of my neck.

But it was carried away
by the sweet-smelling
air of the deep blue Florida night.

Moonlight
gives me courage.

But Eva looked unsure.

Don't worry, Jay laughed.
    You girls will be safe with us.

We're locals, remember? He winked.
    We know what we're doing.

My excitement
was like static electricity.
If anyone touched
my skin,
their hair
would stand
on end.

Yes! I squealed.

In the Dark

Eva and I giggle
and scurry
to the beach house
my parents rented for this trip.

We creep to the glass door,
clutching our sandals,
and

s   l   i   d   e

it

o   p   e   n

ever

so

slowly.

For a moment,
I hold my breath,
wondering if we're about to get busted.

But a sudden burst of
drunken laughter from upstairs
lets me know the coast is clear.

I smile at Eva.

I guess my parents are on vacation too.
Part of me wonders if
they told me to invite timid Eva
so she could keep an eye on me
while they take a break.

In New Dresses

with fresh
lipstick and mascara,
we give ourselves a quick
once-over in the mirror.

I'm shorter and skinnier than Eva.
She says that means I'm prettier.
Her blue sundress is too loose,
skimming over the curves of her body.

Eva's problem isn't her size.
It's her confidence,
or rather lack of it.

One of the only Latina girls
in our school,
she's always stood out
too much for her liking.

Own it! I tell her.
But she shakes her head shyly.

Luckily she found me.
And I have enough
                confidence
for us both.

I look at her
smooth black hair
with envy,

pulling my fingers
through my own
frizzy red mane.

C'mon, I say.
Let's go!

We sneak
back out
to find the boys
at the pier.

My stomach

LEAPS!

Jay takes my hand
to steady me

as I climb aboard
Nate's dad's boat.

The water is
thick and black,
like oil.

It gleams
in smooth waves
that rock us
soothingly.

I rest against
the cool,
white, plastic seat

and
watch

Jay

      undo

      the rope

      that ties us

      to shore.

We Glide

into the open water,
cutting
    swiftly
through
    silky waves.

There are
so many stars
I've never seen before.

I tilt my head back
and watch them scroll by.

I inhale deeply,
savoring the
cool
crisp
clean
ocean air.

I feel Jay's eyes on me
and turn
to see his face
smiling
so very close to mine.

I Met Jay

six hours ago.

When he threw a Frisbee
that almost hit me
as I lay
basking in the sun
like a cat.

I flinched.
Turned to yell,
but my lips curled into a smile
when I saw the tall, good-looking guy
bounding toward me.

He had a mop of wavy, sun-bleached hair
that bounced with each step.
My eyes traced
the smooth lines
of his tanned, shirtless skin.

Sorry! he said, grinning.

But he didn't
look sorry at all.

He was glad
to have a reason
to come talk to me, too.

Arching my back
in my yellow bikini,
I picked up the Frisbee
and fanned myself with it.

Eva snatched
her towel
and covered
herself up.

Nate,
trailing behind Jay,
looked embarrassed.

Like this was a game
he didn't know
how to play.

On the Boat

I watch Eva and Nate
flirting shyly.

Looking at him, I think
he and Jay
couldn't be more different.

Nate's dark, curly hair
is cut short and tidy.

His angular body is awkward,
and his white skin looks too pale
next to Jay's ruddy glow.

Do you get seasick? he asks Eva.

I actually don't know.
It's my first time on a boat,
she tells him.

How is that possible?
He looks shocked.

We're from Pennsylvania,
remember?
I chime in,

laughing
at his confusion.

Yeah, but still…
Nate smiles.

So, what do you guys do for fun? Jay asks.

Eva and I
look at each other,
hesitating.

For Fun:

We study astrology,
giving each other
tarot card readings
and musing about
our horoscopes.

We watch TV
together,
sprawled across
the squashy couch
in my basement.

But right now
these things
don't feel interesting enough
to captivate
Jay and Nate.

So instead I say,
We're both really into music.

Hoping
this makes us sound
cooler than we are.

My Lips

kiss
the rim of a
blue
glass bottle
of gin.

And the warm flush
of alcohol
fills me with fire.

I edge even closer
to Jay,
feeling the heat
of his body
touching mine.

After a Few Drinks

the gin
makes Jay

LOUD

and funny.

He's dancing around,
making the boat shake.

Making us clasp our stomachs,
lose our breath
from laughing so hard.

But the gin
and the waves
must be going to my head.

Everything feels like
it's

t
  u
    r
     n
     i
    n
g

I think I'm seasick! Eva says.

Jay stops dancing,

but

the boat

still

s   a   e
  h   k   s.

The Lights

from the beach
are
        b l u r r y
in the distance.

Is the water moving
        f a s t e r
than it was before?

The slick waves have turned
h e a v y

and

c h o p p y.

They

SLAP

the boat
hard.

They swing

the boat.

One side

flies

UP!

And the other

dips

DOWN.

We Toss

violently.

Water

f
a
l
l
i
n
g

down
on
us.

Falling
from the sky?
Or from the ocean?

The sky and the sea
are the same color.

B L A C K.

It's getting
hard to see

what's above
and below.

Jay is yelling to Nate.

Because suddenly the wind is
                    R O A R I N G.

Lightening splits the sky.

For a moment
we're

i l l u m i n a t e d.

I'm reaching for Eva,
but she's too scared to stand up.

I get on
my hands and knees
and
crawl to her.

Water is everywhere.
The sky pelting us
with rain.

The sea striking us
with waves.

Jay and Nate are trying
to turn the boat
back around.

But in the darkness,
we can't
see the shore.

The Waves

are monsters.

They
T O W E R
and
C R A S H
with a mighty power.

They are alive:
giant black beasts
trying to consume us.

Eva's warm body
hugged tightly
against mine
is the only thing that tells me

this

is

real.

There Is a
Black Wave

coming toward us,
blown by the
raging
wind.

I can smell
the surge of water,
salty and metallic.

And I know

it's coming for me.

The Wave
rears its head
50 feet in the air.

s   p   r   e   a   d   i   n   g,

growing,

until it looms over us.
Blotting out
all sight and sound.

Extinguishing us
in one crushing blow.

I'm Plummeting

deep

deep

deep

down

down

down

I'm suffocating
under the weight
of water in my ears.

In my eyes.

In my mouth,
open,

s   c   r   e   a   m   i   n   g,

NO!

I'm spinning
in the deep.

For the first time
in my life I'm
filled with

D O U B T.

Then,

the sea

spits me out.

Eva

There Are Three

rules of survival.

A person can survive:

        Three minutes without air.

        Three days without water.

        Three weeks without food.

I am gasping

ragged breaths

of icy air.

There Are Two

people flailing

near me in the water.

There Is One

lifeless body

        hanging

broken

        from the boat.

I Dream

about waiters
passing me tumblers
of ice water.

Pearls of condensation

d
r
i
p

down
the sides.

I guzzle

glass
after
glass.

But they
never satisfy
my thirst.

When I wake up,
my throat
is bleeding.

The sides
of my esophagus
are rubbed raw.

My skin feels hot
and too tight.

I spread my fingers

and feel them
sink
into hot,
wet sand.

Someone is

S C R E A M I N G.

I Open My Eyes

to find the scream.

Jay is standing

next to the
shredded pieces
of our boat.

He's staring
at something.

My stomach churns.

I roll to my side
and vomit
an ugly flood of
green and brown.

I try to sit up,
shaking my head
and gagging.

I can see
the shadow
of someone
walking down the beach.

A w a y

from the screams,
and the vomit,
and the wreckage.

Jay,

I croak.
Jay, stop.

His screams
are short bursts
of ugly,
rasping
sound.

He doesn't seem
able to stop himself.

I pull him down
so we're both kneeling
in the sand,
and cover his mouth
with my hand
until
the screaming
stops.

His eyes meet mine,
crusty with sand.

I let my hand fall
from his face.

Who is that?

I ask,

already knowing
the answer.

Brooke's Spine

is broken.

Her body thrown,
            distorted
off the boat.

Brooke who
collects mood rings.

Brooke who
sings loud, shameless karaoke.

Brooke who
wants to be an actress one day.

Brooke,
my brave, beautiful best friend,

is lying

b   r   o   k   e   n

half in the sand.

Like just another piece
of the boat's wreckage.

I don't have
any screams
inside me.

I don't have
any tears.

I just have

this crazy urge
to comb the knots
out of her snarled red hair.

I Start to Crawl

toward Brooke, but
Jay grabs me
and pulls me back.

Don't,
he begs, frightened.
Don't touch her.

I can't leave her there,
says a voice
that doesn't sound like mine.
But it must be, because
I'm the only one talking.

I crawl to Brooke
on my hands and knees.

I'm relieved
that her eyes
are already closed.

I straighten out her dress.
I tidy her hair.

And crawl
backward
away
from her body.

Where Is Nate?

Jay wants to know.

I saw him walking away.
Down the beach,
I tell him.

Where?

I don't know.
I feel blank.
I don't understand
why this matters.

He's coming back. Look.

I lift my heavy arm
and point to a figure
coming slowly toward us.

Nate looks strange.
Or maybe it's my eyes.

His nose is
swollen and bloody.
It looks broken.

Like Brooke's back.

When he crouches beside us,
I reach out and touch it gently.
He winces.

We're on an island,
he says.
I just walked around the entire beach.

   There's no one else here.

Jay and I

stare at him,
not understanding.

What do you mean? Jay sounds angry.

Where are we?
We can't be that far from land.
How long were we out last night?
How far could we have gone?

Nate shakes his head.

I don't know, he says.
I don't remember how far we went out.

You drunk idiot! Jay is yelling.
You got wasted off a few shots of gin.
And now we're lost!

Jay looks like a wild animal.
Like he's going to tear Nate
into as many pieces as the boat.

There was a storm, remember? Nate says.

Or were YOU too drunk to see it?
The tide was too strong to get back.
We could've been carried hundreds of miles away.
You were the one who wanted to go out at night!

You were the one acting like an idiot,
trying to impress a couple of stupid girls!

I don't want
to listen to their anger.
Don't want
to hear them
spew their ugly words.

I might be weak,
I might be silly,
but my Brooke is not.

I crawl back
to Brooke
and hold
her limp hand in mine.

We're not stupid girls.

Jay and Nate

are looking at me
like they're
sorry
and a little bit
afraid.

I didn't mean that,
Nate says.
I'm sorry.
I shouldn't have said it.

Jay takes Brooke's cold hand
out of mine
and gently places it on the ground.
He pulls me back
away from her.

The three of us
look at one another.

Guys,

Jay says.

What're we going to do?

I Don't Bother

to answer Jay.

All I can think about
is Brooke's body
in the sand.

We need to bury her, I mumble.

They both stare at me.

Eva, Nate says.
I don't think we can.

We don't have any shovels.
How would we make it deep enough?

I can't leave her here,
I say flatly.

We'll make a fire, Jay suggests.
I still have my lighter.

I stand up
and start gathering
the pieces
of the boat
into a pile
to burn.

Wait! Nate stops me.
Don't burn it all.

He pulls a
heavy green tarp
out of the wreckage.

We might need some of these things.

When the Pile
Is Complete

I suddenly
don't want

Brooke's body to
       disappear into this fire.

I don't want
to smell her
       crumbling into smoke.

I don't want
to do this last act
that will make her death

       real and final.

But when Jay
pulls the lighter
out of his pocket,
I don't stop him.

He crouches down
and works the
flames
to life,
until they become
a billowing blaze.

The Fire Is
Still Burning

when the sun
begins to fall.

I'm cold but
I don't want to
stand too close
to the ashes of Brooke.

I sit on the beach,
staring out
at the water.

Yesterday it seemed
so inviting.
Today it feels like
something out of
a nightmare.

The two boys
are near the tree line,
talking quietly.

How many hours
have I known them now?

The thought makes
goosebumps erupt

on my
bare arms and legs.

I hug my knees
to my chest,
pressing my face
against them
too hard.

I'm alone,

        I whisper to no one.

Eva

Brooke is
saying my name
in a coaxing voice.

Eva.
Her voice becomes
insistent.
But I don't want
to wake up.

EVA!
she shouts in my ear.

My eyes snap open.

I'm alone on the beach.

It's pitch black.

The kind of

i m p e n e t r a b l e

dark
where you can
hold your hand
inches from your eyes

and see nothing.

The echo of
Brooke's voice
in my dream
is like a punch in the gut.

Like she was
carved out
of my body
and I'm
bleeding openly.

I curl
into a fetal position.
I dig deep
notches into my calves
with my fingernails.

I bite my lip hard

and bury my face in the

grainy sand.

But   I   do   not   cry.

I Know I Will Die

if I can't find water.

The sun is up and
I am already weak
with the need for it.

My thirst is epic.
It overtakes every
thought and feeling
within me.

I remember
watching reality TV
in Brooke's basement.

There was this show
that she loved
where everyday people,
overweight dentists
and pale IT workers,
would leave their cushy lives
to fend for themselves
in a jungle.

The only tools they had
were their brains
and their bodies.
And the winner would get
a grand prize
of $100,000.

Brooke and I would laugh
at their camera confessions,
at their weak wills. We'd say,

We could SO outlast any of these losers.

Walking up the beach,
I laugh bitterly.

Right now I doubt
if I can even stand
one more
minute
without cold,
fresh water
on my tongue.

Nate and Jay

are nowhere
to be seen.

I wander into the jungle,
not bothering
to tell them
where I'm going.

There are palm trees here.
A voice
inside me
is telling me
that palm trees might mean

c o c o n u t s.

I lost my sandals
in the wreck.
The scrubby
growth underfoot
stabs my tender skin.

But my eyes are raised up,

scanning

the tops of the trees
for the heavy,
round bulbs

that could
save me from
this
thirst.

I feel a swooping
kind of *lurch*
in my stomach,

like the thrill of a steep
plunge
on a roller coaster.

Coconuts!

The Tree

is heavy with them.

The fruits are bright green.
Not like the brown coconuts
I've seen at the grocery store.

But I don't care.
I'm going to
get those coconuts
if it kills me.

And looking at this 60-foot tree,
I think it might.

I search the jungle floor
wildly.
Looking for anything
heavy I could throw
to knock down
a coconut.

I pick up rock after rock,
knowing they're too small,
but ferociously pitching them
at the coconuts anyway.

GAAAAAAAHRRRGH!
I scream,
in frustration.

You're going to have to climb it,

           says a nagging voice in my head.

Dried palm fronds
are scattered on the ground.

I gather up the longest pieces
I can find.
I start to
braid them together.

My hands shake
with anticipation.

I push away
thoughts about falling.

        And how are you going to cut them when
        you get up there, hmm?

that familiar inner voice asks.

        You don't even have a knife!

Shut up,

I say aloud.
A first.
I'm not listening anymore.

I stride toward the tree.

I wrap my braided fronds
around the trunk
and around my waist,
and tie them together.

I pull
as tightly
as I can.

I Begin

the climb up the tree.

S   l   o   w   l   y.

Incredibly

s   l   o   w   l   y.

The bark is thorny and barbed.
I clench
my teeth and grab on,
forcing my hands
to clasp it tightly.

I press my feet
against the sides
of the trunk,
moving upward
in an awkward
frog pose.

Pushing

down

with my feet.

Pulling up

with my hands.

As I climb,
I slide my makeshift rope
up with me.
I pretend to believe
that it will catch me
if I fall.

I have never trusted
my body.
Always
a little too big.
A little too different
from everybody else's.
I hid myself in layers.
Lurked in corners.
Tried to make myself

invisible.

But now
there are no eyes to judge me.
And my thirst is overpowering
my self-doubt.

Squeeze.

Push.

Lift.

Grip.

Pull.

Slide.

Inch by bloody inch.
Until I'm halfway up
this stupid tree.

Eva?

I look down.

Major Mistake

My feet lose their grip.
I slide
a precious foot
back down
the trunk.

Jay is standing below me.
Looking horrified.

Sorry! I wasn't trying to scare you! he swears.
Are you okay up there?

I'm fine!
I call down hoarsely.

I feel strangely angry.
And very aware
that my dress
is hitched up
over my hips.
My round legs
splayed ridiculously
around the tree
I'm clinging to for dear life.

Do you need help?
Jay's voice sounds sorry.

But I can't look down
or I'll lose my nerve.

Instead I look straight up.
At the coconuts hanging
above me, tempting me.

I'm fine! I say again.
Can you just...

I want to tell him
to go away.
But I don't want to
hurt his feelings.

Can you just be quiet please?

Sure! Jay is eager to be useful.

Out of the corner of my eye
I can see him
raise his arms up,
like he's ready
to catch me.

I resist the urge
to tell him
I'd crush him.

I heave a sigh.

Okay, focus,

I whisper to myself.

I need to get back on track.
Painstakingly, I climb.

Squeeze.

Push.

Lift.

Grip.

Pull.

Slide.

Until I reach the top.

Green Coconuts

surround me.

They're clustered around
skinny stems.

I secure my hold.
Wrapping my legs
tightly around the tree,
hugging it with
my right arm,
my chest pressed
against it.

I reach my left hand
out carefully.
I grab a coconut.
I tug it as hard as I can
with my one free hand and…
                nothing happens.

I take a deep breath.
Reach out again.
And grab a coconut.

This time, I try
twisting the stem.

I twist and twist

until finally
it breaks free.

Without looking down,
I drop the coconut.

I hear Jay give
a celebratory hoot.

I twist off
as many coconuts
as I can.

Until the muscles
in my legs and arms
are screaming
in protest.

Then I make
the long
trek back down.

Jay Is Freaking Out

He's doing a crazy
fake-tribal dance
around
the pile of coconuts.
Whooping and laughing
in delight.

When I finally
untie myself from the tree,
he scoops me up
in a bear hug.
Spins me
in a dizzying circle.

That was incredible! he shouts.

Why didn't you tell me you had Tarzan skills?
I was losing it down here!
And you're just up there
making it rain coconuts!

I don't know if
I'm woozy or delirious.
But I'm laughing wildly
while Jay shouts:

Coconut Queen.
Eva, Climber of Trees!

My legs are shaking.

I collapse to the ground
in a heap
of laughter and exhaustion.

Lying on the ground,
I try to catch my breath.
Chest heaving, I say,

Oh my God, I'm so thirsty.

Jay looks at me.
And then at the coconuts.

Oh, crud.

The First Thing I Learn

on this island
is that every solution
is followed by
another problem.

Since we don't know how
to open them, Jay and I
decide to take the coconuts
back to the beach.

But then we realize
there are too many for us
to carry in our arms.

Should we make a basket? Jay suggests.

But braiding the palm fronds
for my climbing rope
was just about the max
of my weaving skills.

Without other ideas,
Jay finally
takes his shirt off.
He puts as many coconuts
as he can fit on it.
Holding up the corners
of the hem and sleeves
like a sort of sling.

We carry the rest in our arms
and kick three
back and forth
between us
as we make our way
back to the beach.

Nate

is sitting, bent over
on a big piece of driftwood.
He's drawing
in the sand with a stick.

What're you doing? I ask him.

*I've been trying to
map out our location,*
he says glumly.

*I want to figure out
how far that storm
could have tossed us.*

With a shrug
he drops the stick
to the sand.

Anyway, where were you guys? he demands.

Couldn't you hear us yelling? Jay asks.
*We threw a major party in the woods!
Look, refreshments and everything!*

He balances a coconut
on his palm,
grinning at Nate
triumphantly.

Is that a coconut?
Nate stands and snatches it.
How did you get that?

Jay gives me a
sidelong glance.
He smiles.
Coconut Queen here
shimmied up a tree!

You're kidding me...
Nate's face shows disbelief.

Both of the boys look at me
and suddenly I feel
my face flush red.
My stomach curls
in on itself.
The familiar
u n e a s e
of being
on display.
But also, surprisingly—pride.

So, any ideas of
how to get them open?
I ask Nate.
I keep my eyes down
at the coconut beside my foot.

Actually, yes, he says.
And my eyes snap up.

He's beaming at me.

You See This?

Nate holds up the coconut.

This part's the husk.
We need to get that off first.

Yesterday I told you guys
I walked around the whole island, remember?

Well, there's this one spot I saw.
It was really rocky.
It'll be perfect for cracking coconuts!

Here, c'mon, he says.
He pulls off his shirt
and gathers up the rest of the coconuts.
It's this way.

The two boys are sprinting
down the beach.
But I'm spent
from climbing the tree.

I lag behind, watching
the muscles rippling
under their bare skin.

Jealous

of their careless strength.

My biceps feel tight,
strained from
the morning's effort.
But my arms
still look doughy and weak
compared with the boys'.

I force myself to run.

To catch up with them.

I refuse

to be left behind.

At the Rocks

the landscape is so different

it doesn't even feel like
we're on the same island.

The waves crash
into the rocks,
blasting seawater
high into the air.

I pick my way across
carefully.
My bare feet slipping
on every sharp rock.

Nate finds a rock
he's sure
is sharp enough.
He begins to smash the coconut
against it.

He's hammering
coconut against rock.

Again and again and again.

Until his sweat mixes
with the salt water's spray.

But the coconut

bounces off the rock.
Like it's made of rubber.

Jay and I glance at each other.

*Hey, man....*Jay says quietly,
this doesn't really seem like it's working.

Nate doesn't respond.
He has a stony look
of determination
on his face.

Whack.

Whack.

Whack.

I'm so thirsty I'm ready to drink ocean water.

HA! Jay is yelling.
Yes! You did it, man! You did it!

Nate is silent
as he continues
to strip the husk

off the coconut.
When he's done,
he holds it up again.

Okay! So, see these three little holes?
They're called the eyes.
We have to poke through them
and then we can drink the water.

Nate takes a small, sharp stone
and jams it into the eyes.
He grinds it deep,
hacking into
the fruit.

Finally, he tilts
his head back.
I can see coconut water

c
a
s
c
a
d
e

down the fruit
into his lips.

It takes everything I have
not to
pry the coconut

out of his hands.

Luckily,
he hands it to me.

I close my eyes and let
the sweet water trickle
down my tongue,
into my parched throat.

Nothing has ever tasted so good.

The Three of Us

spend hours
beating coconuts
against the sharp rocks.

I don't care
that my shoulders are aching.

I don't care
that my feet are bleeding.

I don't care
that my body is too big,
too exposed
in my torn sundress.

All I care about
is the sweet coconut juice
that pours into my mouth.
Quenching that terrible thirst.

When I'm too exhausted
to break any more coconuts,
I wander away from the rocks.
Back to the soft sand.

I lay down,
closing my eyes.
Savoring the luxury
of a full stomach.

I can hear Jay and Nate
lay down somewhere
near me.

I don't open my eyes.
But their presence is comforting.
And for a bewildered moment,
I feel strangely happy.

Happy that the three of us are together.

Then with a lurch,
my stomach turns sour.

Because I realize

I already forgot

there should be four of us.

Nate

We've Been on This Island

for three weeks.

That's 21 days.

That's 504 hours.

I do the math in my head
every night
until I fall asleep.

If I don't keep counting,
I might lose track.

I might

f o r g e t.

And I can't
forget.

I can't
give up
on getting out.

I've Heard Stories

about people

                     d i s a p p e a r i n g

off the
Florida coast.

Mysterious cases
of ships and airplanes
going
         radio silent.

      E v a p o r a t i n g

into
500,000 square miles
of ocean
on the 25th parallel.

The triangular stretch between

Bermuda

Miami

Puerto Rico

Logic Tells Me

that these stories
were made up.

That
The Vanishing Place

is just
something whackos
and conspiracy theorists
came up with.
People too eager
to believe in legends
without

PROOF.

I tell myself
it's nonsense.

But the thought of

The Vanishing Place

haunts me.

A ghost
that refuses to die.

I wonder if
I should tell
Eva and Jay
about it.
But I'm afraid
to sound like a fool.

And in any case,
it's hard to picture
Eva's face falling
as I drop
another piece
of unwanted information on her.

So instead,
the knowledge
sticks in my mouth
like cement.

After Weeks

in direct sunlight,
I'm burnt to a crisp.
My once-pasty skin has turned
angry, lobster red.
Even my scalp is scarlet
underneath my curly hair.

I never knew that
skin could feel too tight.
I never knew that
my eyelids could
crinkle in pain.

The others aren't doing
much better.

Eva's brown shoulders
are flaky and peeling.
Jay's dry, chapped lips
will soon be hidden
by his fast-growing beard.

Even our clothes
are beginning
to fall apart.

My belt is too good
a tool to wear.
But if I lose any more weight,
my shorts won't stay

on my hips.

Jay's been living
in boxers since Day Five,
when he decided
it was too hot to
keep wearing his jeans.

Eva's dress
makes me realize
how impractical
most girls' clothes are.

The material is too thin
and tears too easily.

The spaghetti straps
hang on by a thread.
The front is ripped up
from climbing coconut trees.

We all pretend
not to notice.

Every Morning

I take inventory.

Hoping that keeping track
of our supplies
will help me
stay sane.

Right now we have:
▷ one lighter
▷ one tarp (saved from the wreckage)
▷ 15 coconuts
▷ a pile of sharp rocks (20)
▷ a pile of dried palm leaves and sticks (for fire)
▷ 3 shoes (2 mine, 1 Jay's)
▷ 2 shoelaces
▷ 6 palm braid ropes
▷ 1 leather belt (mine)

Every day,
we split up the work
of collecting firewood and coconuts.

Eva and Jay are the better climbers,
so they're usually on coconut duty.
I use my belt to bind together
piles of sticks,
dragging them back to the beach.

At night,
we use Jay's lighter

to start a fire.

When the sun is up,
the heat is almost unbearable.
But the nights here
are surprisingly windy and cold.

I'm dreading the day
the precious lighter fluid
runs out.
We'll have to figure out
how to make a spark
with just rocks or sticks.

Eva had the brainwave of
tying up the tarp on four sticks.
When it rains, we can collect
fresh drinking water.
This helps save us
from our constant thirst.

Our other greatest tool
is bamboo.
On the second day, we discovered
a huge patch of it growing
on the western side of the island.
It took a long time,
but we managed to saw down
some long pieces with rocks.

Jay used another sharp rock
to whittle three crude spears.

We can't live on coconuts, he said.
We need to try to fish.

The Sunlight Winked

off the clear, blue-green waves.

The fish flickered by
in bright flashes of silver.
Swishing speedily past
my ankles.
I could miss them
in the blink of an eye.

Jay, Eva, and I
stood in the shallows,
spaced   out   along
the shore.

The water lapped at my knees.
Stomach rumbling,
I tried to stay as calm and silent
as a stone,
willing the fish
to gather around me.

I held my breath,
the spear aimed and ready
in my hand.

When a long green fish swam past,
I couldn't resist!
I plunged my spear into the water,
stabbing at it blindly,
sending the swarm of little fish

careening away.

My spear came up empty.
Sighing, I waited again.

For what felt like days,
I stabbed at fish after fish.
I came up empty
every time.

Until I accidently
stabbed my foot
with my spear…

I held in a scream,
clenching my teeth together.
Every muscle in my body
tensed as I clutched
my bleeding foot.

After that,
Eva and I gave up.

But Jay stayed
in the water.

After the sun
went down.
After we built our fire.
After we fell asleep.

In the middle of the night
he came
splashing up to camp,

howling like a wolf,
shaking his hair out,
spraying water
all over Eva and me.

By the firelight I could see
him soaking wet,
grinning ear to ear.

He was shivering and holding
up two fistfuls of dead fish!

Suppertime! he crowed,
and tossed
a dead fish at me.

You've gotta
eat your protein
if you want to get strong, boy!
He smacked me
on the arm.

He crouched next to me,
held a fish up to his face
and moved its mouth,
talking in a nasal voice
with this dumb accent:

Please sir, please!
Don't let me die in vain!
Eats me, eats me!

Eva giggled
like he was hilarious.
I laughed, too.

Even though
my foot was throbbing,
dead fish humor
is undeniably funny.

Sometimes It
Seems Impossible

that we've only been here
for three weeks.

In that short time,
I've gone
from barely knowing Eva
to knowing her too well.

I can pretty much tell
down to the minute
when she
gets too hungry.

Her peaceful silence
turns stony.
Her words drip
with sarcasm
whenever she does speak.

I can tell when
she has to pee
but is embarrassed
to tell us.

I see her clench her jaw
and sort of hop-step
as she walks.

I can tell when
she's pretending to sleep.
Her breath a little too controlled,
her eyelids fluttering.

I can see that
she's still grieving for Brooke.
Because she never says her name.

I wonder what Jay sees.

He's My
Best Friend

but sometimes,
it's hard
not to feel annoyed
with Jay.

Since we got here,
I've carried the weight
of being the leader.
Making the plans.
Assigning the work.

You'd think Jay was on
some kind of
tropical vacation.

The way he turns
everything into a joke.
Turns every chore
into a chance
to make Eva laugh.

It must be nice
to shrug off
the responsibility
of the reality checks.

Must be nice
to leave it to me to say:
We need to look for food
when everyone's tired.

To say:
We need to dig a latrine
when Jay whines about diarrhea.

But This Is the Role

Jay's always
made me play.

I've known him
since we were eight years old.

Back home,
he was the clown.

The guy everybody knew
or wanted
to get to know.

I was his
less-interesting friend.

A quiet guy
whose name
didn't stick
in people's heads.

Back then it didn't bother me.

Jay pushed me out
into the world.

And I kept him
grounded.

We were in perfect balance.

Until we were stranded
on this island.

I've Been Working

on getting us rescued.

Jay thinks
all we have to do
is wait.
He's convinced
that rescuers will be
on their way any day.

*They're probably just trying
to pinpoint our exact location,* he says.
Don't worry so much, man!

I wish I could believe that.
But when I think about

     The Vanishing Place,

I'm afraid to wait.

We have to
keep ourselves
active.

We have to stay
in control.

My first plan
was to write

S.O.S.

in the sand.

I convinced the others
to help me
carry big rocks
from one part
of the beach
to another.

But within a day,
a strong tide came in
and covered it all in sand.

My second plan
was to build a huge bonfire
out of dried coconut husks and palm fronds.
The blaze was huge
but short-lived.
The dry husks burned too quickly
and the smoke trail disappeared.

Sometimes it almost feels
like the island
is sabotaging my work.

But I can't start
to think that way.

Or I will lose my mind.

The Raft

is my third plan.
And hopefully the last.

So far I
     drew the design,
     found the right supplies.

It's going to be
smaller and rougher
than I'd like, but oh well.

When all you've got to work with
is bamboo, handmade ropes,
and a tarp, you do what you can.

The base will be made up
of 36 pieces of bamboo.
The eight longest pieces
will be bundled together
in two groups of four.

Then, the 28 shorter pieces
will be bundled into three groups:
two groups of four,
strapped to the ends
of the long pieces,
and one group of 20 in the center.
This will be the floor.

The sail (made of tarp) will go there
and we'll sit around it.

Now I just need to work on
putting it all together.

While I Work

on building the raft,
Eva has agreed to
take over firewood duty.

Jay (unwillingly)
will work on fishing and coconuts.
He's already told me
that the raft idea is stupid.

How are we even going to steer it? he wants to know.

So I add building log oars
to my to-do list.

Eva is
too quiet.
Slow to voice
her opinion.

I know she's afraid
of going back into the water.
I can see in her eyes:
she's picturing
Brooke's broken body on the shore.

I'm tempted not to push her.
But I feel this
sense
of
URGENCY.

They're both
far too
        untroubled.
Too happy
        to wait.

They don't know about

                The Vanishing Place.

Something has to be done.

And I
will have to be
the one to do it.

This raft will be
the rescue
we've all been waiting for.

After Days of Work

the raft
is almost ready.

We'll set sail
tomorrow morning.
Once we've collected
enough fish and coconuts
to keep us fed for a week.

I'm hoping this guess
is more than enough.
That we'll be picked up
within a day or two.

Based on my
basic knowledge
of geography,
I'm guessing we're somewhere
close to the Bahamas.

When I dream
about getting rescued,
I can't help but picture
a huge white cruise ship.
Tourists hanging over the side.
Pointing and gawking at us
on our raft.

I imagine the
TV crews that'll
interview us.
About the
disaster we went through.
And the daring escape
we made.

For once
it'll be

me

in the limelight.

Instead of Jay.

They'll pepper us
with questions.
Demanding to know how
we made it out alive.

And Eva
will look at me
admiringly, and tell them,

It was

          Nate

who saved us.

          Nate

who got us out.

That Night

we have a party
to celebrate
our departure.

We each take turns
asking questions
about what we'll do when we get home.

I can't wait to take a shower,
Eva says.
I think I miss shampoo
more than almost anything.

C'mon, shampoo?! Jay says.
I like your natural musk.

I resist the urge
to roll my eyes.

I'm going to eat,
I say quickly.
I'm buying a chicken finger sub
as soon as my feet hit solid ground.

Jay, what about you? Eva asks.

He takes a moment to think.

Honestly? he says.
I'm going to miss this place.

It takes everything
inside me
not to tell him
he's a fool.

But again,

I hold my tongue.

In the Morning

I'm eager
to get an early start.

But even Eva
seems oddly hesitant.

*What if we never
see this place again?* she asks me.

I hope we never do!

*I know,
it's just that Brooke...* she begins.
*It's kind of like
we're leaving her behind.*

Jay and I
exchange a look.
Neither of us know
exactly what to say.

To break the silence,
I tell them,
*If we don't get going soon,
we're going to have to wait till tomorrow.*

I get into position
behind the raft.
I wait for them
to help me push.

The Raft

is heavy.
The bamboo drags
across the sand.

We

grunt

and
heave

and
push.

Until at last
the water is
lapping at the bottom rungs.

We push it out
as far as we can,
until there's
a drop off in the sand
and our feet can't touch
the ground anymore.

Then we pull ourselves
on board.

Pick up
the log oars
and use them to

propel

     the raft out

         out

            away

               from

                  shore!

We Are on the Raft

for a full day.

Besides our makeshift
tarp sail and log oars,
we have no real way
of directing our course.

We just

         d   r   i   f   t

peacefully.

Hoping the wind
will carry us
back
to
civilization.

At Night on
the Raft

the world

Shrinks.

Or maybe it

ₑₓpand**s**.

The three of us
lean against the sail,
huddled in the center
of the raft.

Everything turns
flat and black.
Flat black sky above.
Flat black sea below.

I'm going to save you,

I want to tell Eva.

I'm going to take you home.

But the darkness
isn't heavy enough
to veil my words from Jay.

I Awake to a Riot of Noises

The flat blue surface
is disturbed
by a pack of
foreign shapes above the water.

There are birds
feeding behind the raft.
Splashing water everywhere.

I can't believe
Jay and Eva
are sleeping
through this racket!

I'm about to wake them up
when I see it.

Something moving
beneath the water.

Something large
swimming
near the back of the raft.

I'm filled with dread.
But can't make myself
look away.

Jay, Wake Up!

I breathe.

Get up, Jay!

Wha...? He's groggy. Slow to understand.

Jay, look!
I point toward
the back of the raft,
where

         the thing

is cutting a
smooth path
under the water.
Unnoticed
by the noisy birds.

What the heck is that?
he asks, alarmed.

I don't know!
I whisper.

We're both on all fours.
Leaning toward
the back end of the raft.
Trying to get a look.

Aaargh! Jay yells and stumbles back.

I see it, too.

A gray dorsal fin
slices through the water
with powerful ease.

Judging from a glimpse
of its tail,
this thing is
at least

                ten   feet   long.

This Isn't Happening!

Jay is saying,
shaking his head.

This can't be happening.

It's happening.
Eva is awake.

She's standing tensed,
her knuckles white
around the fishing spear.

Wait, just wait, I say.

It might go away on its own.
We're not bleeding, right?
Don't you have to be bleeding
for them to try to attack you?

I don't know, man,
Jay says,
staring dumbstruck
at the water.

Don't you remember
that story
from a couple of years ago?
That surfer got bit
for no reason!

But this is real life! I insist.

This isn't the movies!
We are NOT going
to be eaten by freaking sharks!

We're in its feeding area, Eva says.
We don't know
what it's going to do.
Just stay in the middle
of the raft, okay?
Don't let your feet
hang over the side.

This is easier
said than done.
The raft is small
and we have to distribute
our weight carefully.
So we don't put
too much strain
on the ropes.

Jay and I

try to stand up without
rocking the raft too much.

The three of us huddle together
in the center of the raft.

We stare, transfixed,
as the giant animal
slides in and out of view.

With an earsplitting screech,
the birds erupt into the air.

All except one.

The shark's hideous head
emerges from the water,
snapping ferociously
at the poor creature
trapped in its jaws.

Spewing
water,
blood,
and feathers
everywhere.

This Can't Be Happening!

Jay is yelling.

Come on! Eva cries.
Let's get out of here!

She drops the spear
and dips one of the oars
into the water.

Jay grabs the other
and starts rowing, too.

But we're off balance.
The raft is

t e e t e r i n g

from side to side.

Water splattering
across it as it

dips
     d
      o
       w
n

swings

       UP!

dips

       d
       o
      w
      n.

Faster!
Eva's yelling.

*We have to
move faster!*

But neither of them
see what I do.

They're too busy
trying to row
to see

     coming

a   p   a   r   t.

Stop!

I cry.

We're breaking the raft!

Eva and Jay freeze.

We can't see
the shark anymore.
But the bird's scarlet blood
is blossoming in the water
only feet away.

The reality of
our situation
hits me.
Like a brick in the face.

My raft is

s p l i n t e r i n g

into pieces.

There is a shark
in the water
underneath us.

I have no idea where we are.

Then Somehow

a miracle:

        the   island   appears.

Almost as if

        it heard my thoughts.

Almost as if

        I willed it into existence.

I Can See the Island!

Eva shouts.

I can see it!
We can get back!
Come on, keep rowing!

That's impossible!
I tell her,
even though
I can see it, too.

How
can we be back

after traveling
a day and a night?

It doesn't make sense.

Uninvited,
thoughts about

The Vanishing Place

t
r
i
c
k
l
e

into
my
mind.

NO,
I say forcefully.
It's impossible!

It doesn't matter, Jay cries.

Let's just get
out of here before
that thing
decides it's
snack time again!

The Two of Them

start rowing again.

Meanwhile,
I dart around
behind them.
Desperately trying
to repair
the back
of the damaged raft.

I need to
lash the bamboo rods together.
Before we

c a p s i z e

completely.

I slice my hands
on the unraveling
palm ropes.
Weaving and
knotting them.

Pulling with
all my strength.
Tying the
disconnecting pieces
back together.

Blood Is Streaming

down my hands.
The salt water
licking
my wounded skin.
But I can barely feel the sting.

All my energy
is <u>focused</u>.

                              I have to fix this.

I don't notice

the shark

                m a t e r i a l i z e

in the water

beneath me,

until

it's

too

late.

I Don't Have Time

to SCREAM.

I'm falling
off the raft.
Plunging
into the ocean.

My mouth
fills with water.

Every cell
in my body

is

SHRIEKING.

But

I can't call out.

I can't think.

I can't see.

I'm flailing
in the water.

I can't grab

the raft.

I'm sinking and

I know

I'm going

to die.

Someone

plummets into the water.

It's Eva.

She dives into me.
Grabs me
around the middle.
Tries to pull me up.

On the raft,
Jay is jabbing his fishing spear
at the shark.
Trying to keep it away
from us.
Stabbing at it
as it thrashes wildly.

I kick
as hard as I can.
Pushing myself
to the surface.
Frantically trying
to breathe.

In the frenzy,
something huge
slams into me.
It knocks me HARD
into the raft.

There's a moment of
head-splitting pain.
A burst
of scarlet light.

And then

       everything

             fades

                  out.

When I Wake Up

we're on shore.

Eva is kneeling beside me.
When she sees that I'm awake,
she collapses in the sand.

Jay is doubled over,
coughing and spluttering.

Trembling,
I stuggle to sit up.
My head is pounding.
Dizzy, I almost fall back down.

What happened? I croak.
My throat is raw.
My ribs are aching
with every breath.

The shark,
it knocked you out,
Jay says.

It's only then
that I realize
he's bleeding
into the sand.

Did it get you? I ask, horrified.

He smiles weakly.
It tried.
The skin on his hands
is tattered and bloody,
but the cuts
don't seem too deep.

Jay stabbed it with the spear,
Eva tells me shakily.
It was incredible.

Even now I feel
a twinge of jealousy
at her words.

It's me,
not Jay,
who's going to save us.

We need to rebuild the raft,
I say,
looking around for the pieces.

We lost a few of the bamboo rods.
And most of the binding
has come undone.
But from what I can see,
it can be fixed.

Jay looks at me
like I'm insane.

Are you crazy? he asks me.

I'm Not Crazy

I say defensively.

We need to get out of here.
We have to move
as quickly as possible.

Neither of them
will look me in the eye.

Man, give it up, Jay mutters.
It's time.

Time for what? I demand.

Hot waves of blood
are pounding in my ears.
I can feel the panic rising
inside of me.

What is it time for? I ask him again.

Jay's eyes are direct,
almost fierce.

It's time to face facts.

We can't keep doing this to ourselves.
You could've died today.

We all could have.

We're not going to get out of here.
Not on a raft.

We're just going to kill ourselves trying.

I Don't Want

to hear this.

I don't want
to have this
conversation.

Not now.

Not while
I'm still reeling
from the shark attack.

Not while
my head
is throbbing
with a
sickening pain.

If we give up, I begin slowly,

we're never going to get out of here.

You don't understand.

No one is going to find us.

Stories about

The Vanishing Place

eat at my mind.

Eva stares at me.
What are you talking about? she asks.

I don't know
how to explain.
How can they
not see?

If

                          The Vanishing Place

is real,
we're going to be
lost forever.

I'm gripped
by a fresh wave
of terror.

We CAN'T stay here!
I scream at them.
*I'm not going to die
in this place!*

Would it really be so awful?
Jay whispers.

He Actually
Says This

Out loud.

For a moment,
I'm speechless.

Then the panic
I've been
suppressing
since we got here
erupts into

RAGE.

Yes.
Yes, it would be awful!
I spit at him.

Are you freaking
kidding me?
You want to spend
your life on this
godforsaken island?

Jay still doesn't look up.
I want to kick sand
into his downturned eyes.

Right now I hate

everything about him.

I hate his too-long hair.

I hate his tattered boxers.

I hate his ridiculous sense of humor.

I hate his weakness.

I Can't Stop

the words
that come pouring out
of my mouth.

Of course you want to stay here
you idiot, you loser,
I snarl.

You're not such
a failure here, are you?

You love this dump!
You're king of the
freaking island!
You piece of trash.

I laugh.

You're nothing!

You think I need you?

You think WE need you?

You are completely

WORTHLESS.

A Sound
Escapes Me

like an animal's growl.

And before I know
what I'm doing
I'm on top of Jay,

shoving him
into the sand,

pummeling his face
with my fist.

Eva is screaming
words I can't make out,

trying to pull me
off of Jay.

He's not even
trying to fight back,

but I'm still yelling:

Trash! You no-good piece of trash!

You did this, didn't you?

You got us stranded on purpose!

There's a walloping blow
to the side of my head
as Jay hits me
for the first time.

I blink and spit blood
out of my mouth.

Now he's on top of me,
his knees pinning
my torso down.

He's looking
at me like
he's never
seen me before.

What did you say? he asks.

I said YOU did this.

You got us lost
here on purpose.
You just wanted to escape
your miserable life
and you took us
all down with you!

This is all your fault.

You killed us all.

I Don't Know

if I mean it.

But right now
I don't care.

It feels so good
to blame Jay.

It feels so good to
punish him
for flirting with Eva.

It feels so good
to finally let go.

It feels so good
to have a

          rational explanation

for why we're stranded here.

I'm Waiting

for him
to punch me again,

but he doesn't.

He stumbles off me,
staggering
to his feet
like he's drunk.

Eva looks horrified.

She's standing
above me,
red-faced,
mouth open.

Her eyes darting
from

        me

        to

        Jay.

Jay is
backing away
from us.

Tripping backward
in the sand.

Until his feet
touch the water.

He looks up
at us blindly.

Then leaps into
a full-speed run
into the jungle.

Jay

Was It True?

Did I cause the wreck?

Did I get us lost?

Did I kill Brooke?

Have I killed us all?

I try to remember
how much I drank,
how far we drifted.

But that night
on the boat
feels like something
out of someone else's life.

Something
I dreamed.

What came

b e f o r e

hasn't existed

since I woke up
in the sand.

Since that first breath

      told me

I was still alive.

What Does
It Matter

how we got here,
and why?

I learned
from my mom:

if you want to survive,

if you want to forgive,

you

f o r g e t

what came before.

You focus
on the

n o w.

You focus
on what's

r e a l.

What's

h e r e.

What you can

t o u c h.

I choose
to forget
when I was a kid.

The weeks
she left me
alone.
Locked in
the apartment.
Eating cereal
and watching TV
for days.

I choose
to forget
her fits of drunken rage.

Slinging abuse,
calling me *trash*.
Beating me
black and blue,
on top of yellowing bruises
that had just barely healed.

She Said

there was

    no point

    dwelling
    on the past.

Asking where she was.

Or who she was with.

Or why I couldn't come.

    No point

    whining about
    things that already happened.

She said each day was

    a new beginning.

And we would
wipe our slates clean
and start fresh.

So that's what I did.

I pushed the past
                    away.

Until it faded,
almost

              d i s a p p e a

I did it
every time she left.

Every time
she came back.

Every time
she hurt me.

Every time
she sobered up.

So what's *the point*
of asking

WHY this happened to us?

All you can do
is
make the best
of the situation.

Make the best
of
being alive.

I'm Alone

in the jungle.

I ran until
I couldn't run
anymore.

And now
I'm standing
in the pitch black.
The jungle of trees
blotting out the starlight.

I stand and breathe.
Letting the
waves of pain
wash over me
like water.

They ripple
through my body.

One   after   another

and I wait
for them to pass.

But a nagging doubt
keeps them flowing.

Nate's Not Wrong

I was a failure
back home.

D's in all my classes.
I was going nowhere.
Except maybe the same place
as my mom.
Chasing one
bender with another.

I had nothing.

I was the good-time guy.
And people liked me
in a shallow kind of way.
Without knowing much
of anything about me.

Nate was the only one
who knew my secret.
Knew about my mom.
Knew that I was trash
pretending to be cool.

The betrayal of his words
aches more than my bruises.

I Had Never Felt

like I had a *purpose*
before I came to the island.

As strange
as it sounds,
I feel like I *belong* here.

It's only in this
forgotten place
that I ever had
value.
Or imagined
that I did.

I like
the way it feels
to face
each test of survival
and win.

I like falling asleep
        to the sound
        of the ocean.

Waking up to
        the sunrise.

Living each day
        FREE.

From taunts.
From abuse.
From pain.

Living each day
          in peace.

I don't waste my time
wondering where we are.
Or how we got here.

I just feel...
          grateful.

I said I wanted
to wait for a rescue.
But truthfully,
I've pictured
what it would be like
to spend my life
on this island.

To feel
Eva's skin
against mine.
To breathe in
the coconut smell
in her hair.

To be free
from what's
waiting for me
back home.

In the Real World

I was
n o t h i n g.

When Mom hit me,
I used to close my eyes.

I pictured
my body disappearing
into nothing.

I wished that I could

               v   a   n   i   s   h

from the face of the earth.

As the Sunlight

begins to filter
through the trees,
I know
what I have to do.

The lethargy
I once felt
at home in my cluttered apartment
is replaced
with energy.

Energy
I never knew
was inside me.

For once I'm filled
with purpose.

For once I'm filled
with confidence.

I make my way
back to the beach.

Nate's Face

is ghostly.

He's working obsessively.
Trying to put the raft back together.
He's racing around,
throwing broken pieces away.
His bloody hands yanking
the heavy boards back into place.

Eva is sitting nearby,
braiding palm fronds
into ropes.

*You can take the raft
and go,* I say loudly.
*I'm not going
with you.*

Eva looks stunned.
She stands, dropping
the rope.
She turns
to look at Nate.

Nate throws down
a bamboo rod angrily,
sending it clattering across the raft.

No. Nate is shaking his head.
You can't stay here.

Taking the raft
is our only hope.

I know what this place is.
We couldn't send back
a rescue for you.

We have to go together.

If you stay here,
you're never going
                    to be found.

I look him
straight in the eye.

I know him so well.
And even after everything
he said last night,
he doesn't want
to let me go.

I know, I tell him.
And I don't care.

I'm Not Going

to fight this anymore.

I'm here.
I'm alive.
I'm going to stay alive.
I'm not leaving
this island.

For a long moment,
we stare at each other.

We both understand
what this will mean.

I can't... Nate says.
I'm sorry, Jay.
I have to get out of here.

Eva is looking
helplessly

from Nate   to me   and back again.

When we both turn to her,
her face crumples.

She sinks to her knees,
her hands in her hair.

I Go to Her

before Nate can,
dropping to the
ground beside her.

Gently, I place my hand
on her head, stroking her hair.

Eva,
I whisper.
It's going to be okay.

She tilts her head up,
looking at me.
Her brown eyes
filled with sadness.

I continue to stroke her hair,
looking back at her steadily.

Everything inside me
is willing her
to understand.

*I want you to go
if you want to.
I'm going to be fine.*

In an instant, her lips are on mine.

Her Arms

wrap around me,
her hands
in my hair.

Her body is pressed
against me,
almost pushing
me down.

I can't breathe.

There are fireworks

e x p l o d i n g

in my stomach,

in my brain.

YES!

Oh my god.

Yes.

This is everything.
Everything I've been wanting.
Everything I've been waiting for!

But a small voice,
somewhere in
the back of my mind,
(a voice that sounds like Nate's),
is telling me

NO.

Tenderly,

I put my hands

on her shoulders

and push her

away.

Eva

There Are Three

of us standing
on an empty beach.

There are two
friends staring at me,
waiting for an answer.

There is one
person who can
make this choice.

This Time

there is no Brooke
to answer for me.

There is no Brooke
to make me brave.

There is only me.

And I will decide
what my own fate will be.

I'm Not Going

to make this
a decision

                        between

               Nate   and   Jay.

I couldn't choose
between them
without breaking
my own heart.

Instead,
I'm going to decide
what I want
for my own future.

If I Stay

can I turn my back
on the world
waiting for me?

Can I make
a life here?

In some ways,
I am happy here.

This place
has made me
into someone new.

Someone strong,
capable,
and independent.

Someone

                    unafraid

of being seen.

If I Go

there is a whole world
waiting for me.

But there's a chance
that I could die
before I even
make it there.

Is it better
to make a life here?

Or is that giving up?

It Will End

with a *Yes!*

A *yes* to one choice

and one choice only.

Nate's gentle brown eyes
look into mine searchingly.

I can see he's afraid
of losing us both.

Jay watches me
with a strange
calmness.

He stands and moves away,
giving me space
to make up my mind.

I'm Going

on the raft,
I tell them.

I have to be brave.

And for me,
staying here
wouldn't be bravery.
Although maybe it is
for Jay.

I will never try
to be invisible again.

Nate

seems stunned
and incredibly relieved.

We'll try to send a rescue boat
when we make it back to shore,
he says to Jay.

Once we're found.
I promise
we won't leave you here to die.

But Jay is shaking his head.
You know you don't believe that.

Jay comes back to me.
But I can't bear to say goodbye.

Please believe me, he whispers,
it's better this way.

I wrap my arms around him,
burying my face in his warm neck.

There are no words
for what I'm feeling.
No words to give him
to hold on to.

I'll never forget you,
I tell him.

Nate

When It's Time

to send the raft out,
Jay helps us
carry the weight.

Side by side, we push together.
Until waves begin to pull
the raft into the tide.

A heavy wind blows,
filling the sail.

Eva and I climb onboard
and take up the oars.

Jay, standing waist-deep
in the water,
holds up his hand, waving goodbye.

Godspeed! he says jokingly.

We'll send back help,
I say again.
Just stay alive,
will you?

You too, bud.
Jay smiles.
Take care
of our girl.

The Wind

is picking up.
Carrying the raft
out to sea.

The thick waves
are pulling us

        out...

                and out...

                        and out...

Too soon,
Jay is nothing more
than a speck in the distance.

He fades
as we sail

        away....

                away...

Eva and I

don't speak.

The reality of leaving Jay behind
weighs too heavily on us both.

This time on the raft
is nothing like the last.

No excited anticipation
of what's to come.
No peaceful, dreamy
floating toward a brighter future.

The water
seems to reflect
my dark mood.

The waves are fierce and choppy,
slapping the raft back and forth.
The wind pounds the tarp,
pulling the sail first one way,
then another.

I use all of my strength
to pull on my oar,
trying to keep us on a straight course.

Soon

it begins to rain.

Droplets spatter
against the tarp noisily,
hitting our faces,
stinging us.

The sky begins to darken,
gray clouds consuming
the open blue.

I can feel
the bamboo rods shifting
beneath my feet.
But I don't look down.

Instead,
I look at Eva.

For the First Time

she is crying.

The tears stream down
her crumpled, red face.
Mixing with the rain
that's beating down on us now.

Lightning
splits the sky
with an almighty

CRACK

and I jump.
Feeling the rods

r o l l

beneath my feet.

It is the storm.
All over again.

But this time,
it's my fault.

This time
I know
we don't really
stand a chance.

I Turn to Her

in agony.

I'M SORRY!

I scream
over the wind.
But my words
are drowned out
by the uproar of thunder.

The sky is an evil shade

of **B L A C K**

I begin to shake
uncontrollably.

Without meaning to,
I drop my oar.

In an instant,
it's carried away
by the vicious waves.

There Is

a dark wave,
creeping toward us.

I can see it

mounting in the distance.
Consuming each smaller wave,
taking them into itself,

g r o w i n g

and

g r o w i n g

as it rolls ever

closer.

And

closer.

And
closer
toward us.

There Is Nothing

left to do
but wait.

There is nothing
left to do
but let go.
Give in.
Finally.

I fall to my knees,
pulling Eva down.
Grasping the base
of the sail with one hand,
her body with the other.

Eva's sobs
shake her body.
I press my lips
against her cheek, hard.

This all is my fault,
I scream in her ear.
Not knowing if
she can hear me
through the deafening wind.

Eva shakes her head.
But it doesn't matter.

Now, there is no escape.

For One

spine-chilling instant,
the wave rears up.

It rises,
hanging above us,
as though
considering its prey.

Eva and I
cling to each other
for dear life.

It crashes down
on our tangled bodies.

Driving us

deep

deep

deep

into
the freezing
water.

Underwater

I'm ripped
apart from Eva.

I flail blindly,
somersaulting in the churning water,
until at last
I'm tossed upward.

I choke,
swallowing saltwater.

I can't see Eva anywhere.

The darkness is incredible.
I spin in a circle,
squinting to see through the rain.

Wave after wave
pulls me under
and I have to fight
with every ounce of strength
I have to get back up.

Another bolt of lightning
tears across the sky,
and for a split second
I can just make out
the shape of the island.
The shape of
                    The Vanishing Place.

Jay

From the Shore

I watch the raft
disappear into the horizon.

Knowing I will
never see them again.
Knowing I will
spend the rest of my life
alone,
wondering
if they ever made it back.

A deep chill
creeps through my veins.
I start to shudder.

Rubbing my arms,
I gather up firewood,
piling it in our usual spot.

I pull out my lighter
and flick it on.
The bright flame bursts into life,
but in a moment it's
blown out
by a gust of wind.

I try again.

Again the wind
douses the flame.

In Horror

I look up at the darkening sky.
Droplets of rain begin falling
on my upturned face.

My stomach clenches.
They're not going to make it,
says a voice in my head.

I push it away.

But I have to do something.
Maybe if I got higher,
I could see further out.

I race into the jungle,
making my way toward
a steep ridge I saw once
while collecting coconuts.

I launch myself onto it,
digging my hands into the earth.
Growling, I wrench myself upward.

The tumult of rain
beats down on me,
making me slip,
covering me in mud.

Panting, I finally haul myself
onto the top of the ridge.

I blink the rain
out of my eyes,
wiping my face.

Searching
over the tree line
for a sign
of my friends out at sea.

My heart drops.

I can see someone
near shore.

Someone

                    f l o a t i n g

facedown in the water.

Furiously

I stumble and slide
back down the ridge.
I race to the beach.
Fling myself into the water.

I'm attacking the waves.
Beating my way toward him.
Each wave hammers me like a club.
Every muscle in my body
screams in protest.

I reach Nate, pulling him up.
Roll him onto his back.
Under the dusky sky, his face looks blue.

His head lolls
limply on my shoulder.
I don't know
if he's dead or alive.

With Nate heavy in my arms,
I search for Eva.

I close my eyes and pray.
To anyone. To anything.

When I open my eyes,
I see her.

She is swimming toward the shore.

WANT TO KEEP READING?

If you liked this book, check out another book
from West 44 Books:

CLEAR CUT
BY MELODY DODDS

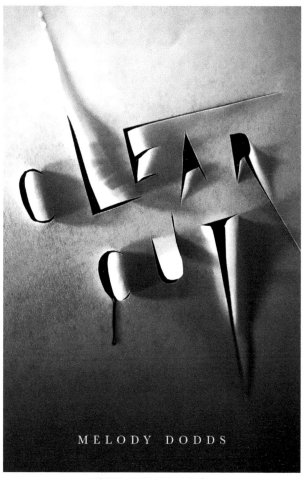

ISBN: 9781538385142

SICK

They found Josie
in the locked bathroom
of a Bar Harbor café.

She had cut herself.

Her blood seeped
under the door.

I like to think
that it couldn't
        ever
have been me.

I would never be
        that careless,
            that sad,
                that sick.

I *like*
to think that.

HEATHER WRIGHT – ALWAYS ALRIGHT

Through rain
    and snow
        and dark of night.

And never-ending
parent fights.

                    It's all good.
                    It's perfect.

I've got
Chairman Meow
to purr
    and cuddle.

I've got my best friend,
Liv,
to gossip
    and giggle.

                    It's fine.
                    It's terrific!

My parents yell
    and I tell
        jokes about it.

DID YOU HEAR THE ONE ABOUT...

the lobster fisherman
who spent
all his money
on his wife's
college degree?

He was CRABBY
about it,
but at least
they didn't need to see
a PRAWNbroker!

And he *did* believe
that education
was SHR-IMPortant.

So he agreed
to going broke
by SHELLING out money
for everything
all those years.

But now,
his wife says
she thinks
that the lobsterman
doesn't do enough

and also
that he may be having
a SQUID-life crisis.

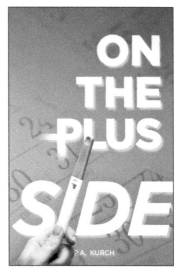
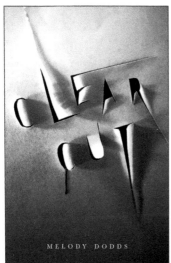

CHECK OUT MORE BOOKS AT:
www.west44books.com

An imprint of Enslow Publishing

WEST **44** BOOKS™

About the Author

Theresa Emminizer is a writer and editor from Buffalo, New York, where she earned her degree in history and creative writing. She is the author of several educational nonfiction books including *HMS Beagle Voyage and the Galápagos Islands*. She enjoys traveling to new places, wandering in nature, and spending time with her husband and cats. This is Theresa's first novel.

.